THE LOST CARNIVAL

THE LOST CARNIVAL
a dick grayson graphic novel

written by MICHAEL MORECI
illustrated by SAS MILLEDGE with PHIL HESTER
colored by DAVID CALDERON
lettered by STEVE WANDS

THE LOST CARNIVAL

DC Comics, 2900 West Alameda Ave., Burbank, CA 91505
Printed by LSC Communications, Crawfordsville, IN, USA. 3/27/20. First Printing.
ISBN: 978-1-4012-9102-0

Library of Congress Cataloging-in-Publication Data

Names: Moreci, Michael, author. | Milledge, Sas, illustrator. | Hester, Phil, 1966- illustrator. | Calderon, David, colourist. | Wands, Steve, letterer.
Title: The lost carnival : a Dick Grayson graphic novel / author, Michael Moreci ; illustrator, Sas Milledge with Phil Hester ; colorist, David Calderon ; letterer, Steve Wands.
Description: Burbank, CA : DC Comics, [2020] | Audience: Ages 13+ | Audience: Grades 10-12 | Summary: Before Batman trained him to be Robin, Dick Grayson was star of his family of trapeze artists, but when an enchanting new attraction opens nearby and threatens to lure away their remaining customers, Dick is among those drawn to its magical glow and may be too mesmerized to recognize the dangers ahead.
Identifiers: LCCN 2020000770 (print) | LCCN 2020000771 (ebook) | ISBN 9781401291020 (paperback) | ISBN 9781779504180 (ebook)
Subjects: LCSH: Graphic novels. | CYAC: Graphic novels. | Carnivals--Fiction. | Aerialists--Fiction. | Magic--Fiction. | Family life--Fiction.
Classification: LCC PZ7.7.M658 Lo 2020 (print) | LCC PZ7.7.M658 (ebook) | DDC 741.5/973--dc23
LC record available at https://lccn.loc.gov/2020000770
LC ebook record available at https://lccn.loc.gov/2020000771

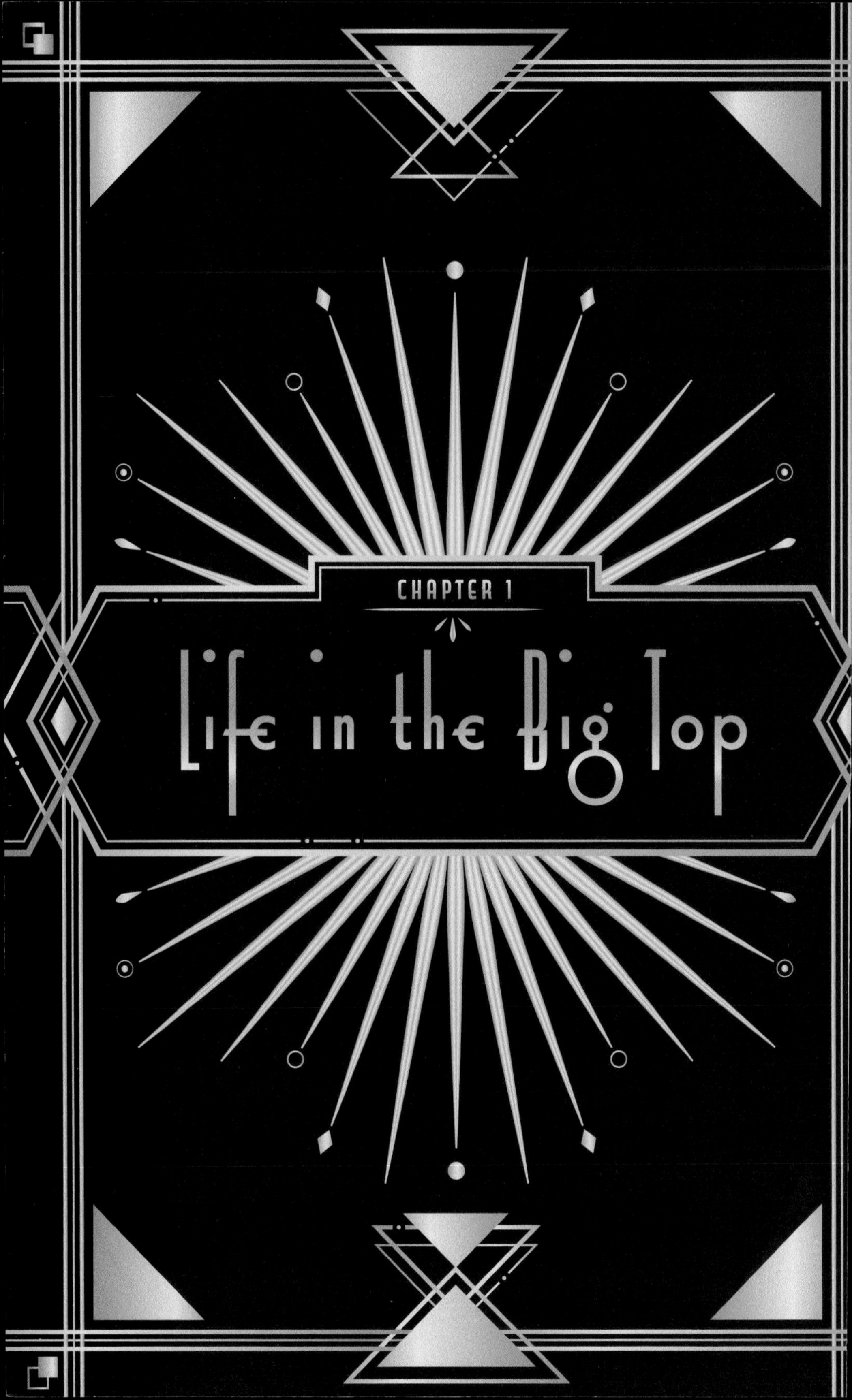

CHAPTER 1

Life in the Big Top

HALY'S CIRCUS.
OUTSIDE CHEYENNE, WYOMING.
JUNE.
Haly's
Haly's
"Ladies and gentlemen, boys and girls!
"You've traveled from across the city...
"Across the county, across the state, and beyond.
"And you've come for *one* reason..."

To be *amazed.*

From Boise to San Antonio, Missoula to Muncie, they have dazzled audiences with their breathtaking feats that defy gravity so profoundly you'll leave thinking man can *fly.*
They give something this modern world cannot—*wonder.*
Prepare to be astonished, prepare to be thrilled as Haly's Circus proudly presents the unparalleled, the unrivaled, the one, the only...

THE FLYING GRAYSONS!

Another low turnout, Dad.
Don't worry about the crowds. Worry about the routine.
I gave up my summer for the routine. It'd be nice if people were here to see it.
Hey, at least the circus *only* travels in the summer.
Otherwise you'd be a full-time carny like your mother and father.
Right. As if that's not where my life is heading anyway.
I'm just having some fun, Dick.
Let's get this show started on one, two...

Three!

Ladies and gentlemen, there he flies!
But!

"Will...
"He...
"Make it?"

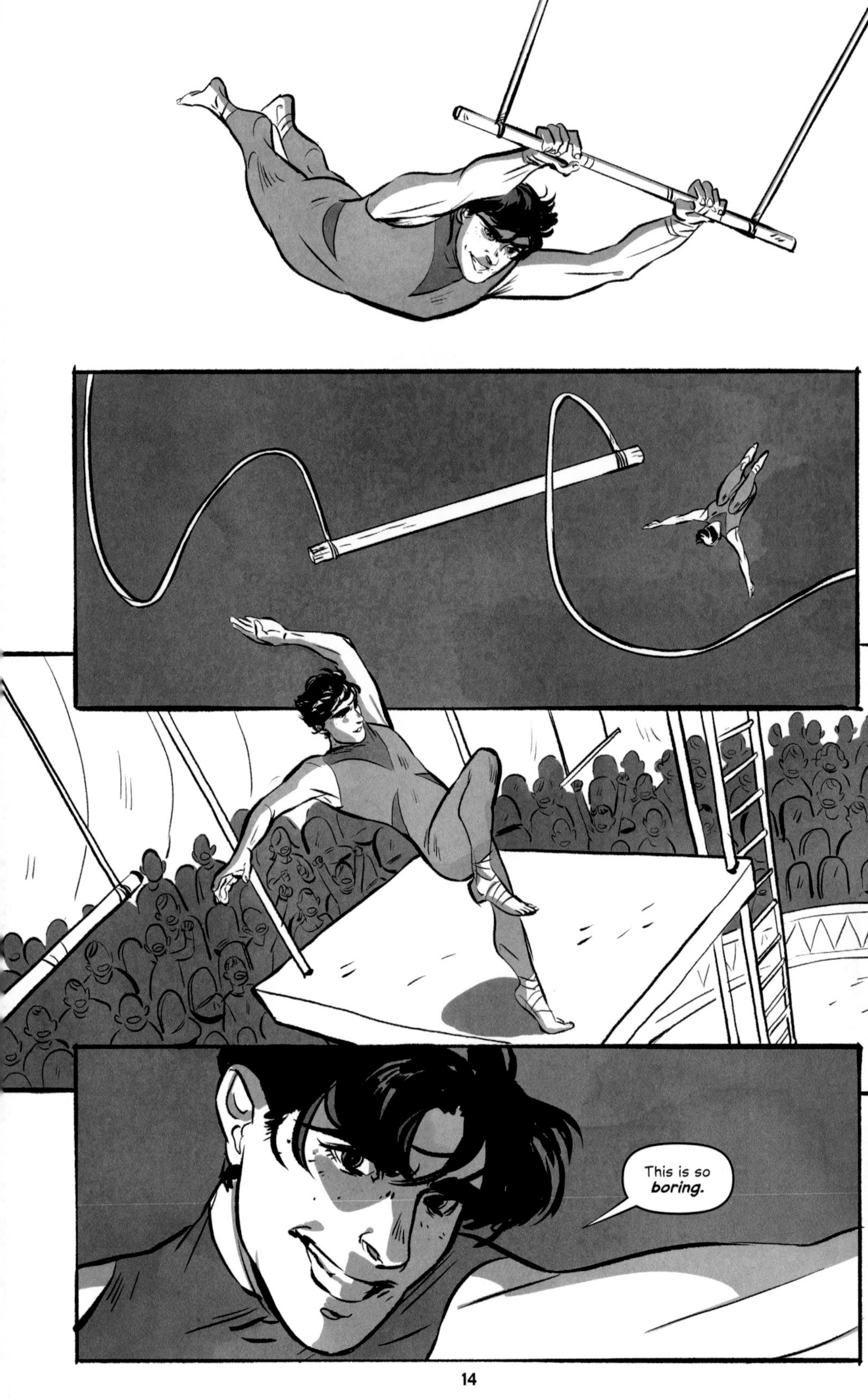
This is so
boring.

Are
you ready,
folks?

Let's close this show with a bang.
Really? You're calling this a ***bang?***
This is our ending. You want to design a finishing routine, be my guest.
All right. Maybe I will.
Nice and easy. Get to Mom, hit an aerial somersault, and—
Dick? Are you listening?

Hey—
what are you
doing?!
Don't you
do this. Do **not**
go off script.
Damn it,
Dick!
What are
you—
"Ladies and gentlemen!
You came here to be
astonished! You came
here to be awed!"

And the stupendous, death-defying ***Flying Graysons*** delivered!

BACKSTAGE.

What in the world was ***that?!***

You think our business is in a golden age, Grayson? We're getting squeezed by the internet, pushed around by that "Cirkay Solay", and every town we hit is ***broke.***

Need I remind you how many people this circus employs? How many lives would be affected if your act tanked?

Think about how happy you'll be as *unemployed* acrobats.
This is no different from when he was five, and we had to tell him the same thing over and *over.*
I don't remember him *choosing* to be so stubborn. Nothing I say gets *through* to him.
Then maybe you shouldn't say anything. Maybe you should *listen* instead.
Well, you're just filled with crazy ideas, aren't you?
All right, Dick—talk to me. Tell me what's on your mind.
Right. Because you're interested in what I have to say.
I'm here, aren't I?
But I don't want to be here, Dad, doing the same routine for the same bored crowds.
I just want things to change.
Haly's

This is our *life.* This is what we do, all of us. It's how we survive.
And sometimes, there are things happening that are bigger than what we might want. Look over here—
More competition. A carnival.
That's why Mr. Haly's even tenser than usual.

All I see is another reason why the things I want don't matter.
I don't have time for this. There's work to do around here, and I still have to run to town for groceries.
Haly's
I'll go.
C'mon, Dad. Let me have some time to... clear my head.
Fine, you can go. But, and I mean this: right to town and back. That's it.
Absolutely, Dad...

"Right to town and back."
Willow! Hey, Willow! Hop in!
Uh—**no.** See, unlike **some** people, I prep for my shows.
Come on, you don't have a show for **hours.** Let's get out of here—I promise, I won't get you into **any** trouble.
14-H35
Oh, you won't. Because if there **is** trouble, I'll just blame it all on you.
You know you'd be lost without me. Besides, we're just going on a nice drive to town.
Dick Grayson, thank goodness you have your looks, because you're a **terrible** liar.
VWWRRRMMMMM

OUTSIDE THE CIRCUS, GREATER WYOMING.

So tell me—what are these great expectations of yours?

I mean, you keep going on about how you're too good for the circus—

I never said *that.*

Okay. But we're, like, three weeks into summer, and all I've heard you talk about is wanting to get away. I think it's fair to ask where you want to go.

Everything has its ups and downs. Why do you think I practice my magic so hard? You think I want to be my crazy uncle's understudy my whole life?

One day, I'm going to be the best magician there is. Famous—and *rich.* And I won't *need* Haly's.
Better not let your uncle Lodz hear you talking like that. You and your ambition will be out in a heartbeat.

Pfft. Sure. You *try* to find someone to put up with that grump. Besides—I'm going to be *better* than Lodz.
Hey, know what I heard? There's a party at this place, Miller's Ravine. Which just *happens* to be a little ways ahead.
Nope.

Come *on.* Think about how bummed I've been.
We'd be in so much trouble.
If anyone found out. Which they won't.

Fine. But if we get busted, I'll turn you into a rabbit. Then you'll be in all my acts, and you'll spend your rabbit life watching me become awesome.

MILLER'S RAVINE.
Okay, we came. Can we go now?
Willow, part of going to a party is ***going to a party.*** Don't you want to feel like a normal teenager? For ten minutes?
First of all, I feel fine. Second, townies tend to like us circus people when we're on stage. Not when we're inserting ourselves into their lives.
You're overthinking things. These are just kids like us. If we just gave them a chance, I'm sure—
Yo, carny!
You were saying?

Just ignore them, okay? We're **leaving.**
Aw, c'mon, carny. Don't leave...
We just wanna have some fun.

Dick, don't do it. ***Doooooon't*** do it.
You realize telling me not to do it makes me want to do it even more, right?
Yeah, kinda.
Haly

You are one ***ugly*** freak, even by carny standards. They keep you around to make the bearded lady look good?

I'm talkin' to you, Scarface. You best spit out an answer or—
Enough already! We said we're leaving. We'll go back to our carnival and you'll never see us agai—
And I said I'm having a chat with my new friend, so get the ***hell*** out of my ***face.***
HEY!

Heads up, meathead.
OOOOOF!
Who are you—and what are you *doing?*
Uh, you're ***welcome.*** But I hadn't planned anything past kicking that guy in the face.
Well, think ***fast.***
Always.

AAAHHHH!
oOOOOOF!
Where you gonna go, carny? Ain't nowhere to run.
Who said anything about runni—
Hey! **Hey!**
Get off of me! Get ***off***—

Why? Things are just about to get **good.**
After all...
I'm a little princess who wants to be pretty in pink.
What did I just say?
Ow!
POW
What the—
Uh, Chase, bro, you okay?
Yes. I'm—

FINE!
OOOOFF!
Look, man, I don't even know.
Yeah— we're out.
Maybe you'd feel better if you came to my tea party?
What... how... what?
Dick!
We need to get out of here.
Willow, we're from the circus and this is the weirdest thing I've ever seen. And where'd that girl go?
Haly's

Shouldn't we check to see if the boy who helped you is—
Luciana, we *can't.* We need to get you *back.*
Hey! Hold up a second.
You *again?* Look, thank you. Okay?
What? No—I don't care about that. I want to know about the *other* thing.
Oh, um, *that...*
Yeah, the hands. What was that thing you were doing with your hands?

Well, it was...
Amazing.

Really? Because most people are a little...weird about it.
We have to **go.**

I have to see her again.
Of course you do.
For now, though, we need to leave before you get carried away...

"But I can tell it's ***way*** too late for ***that.***"

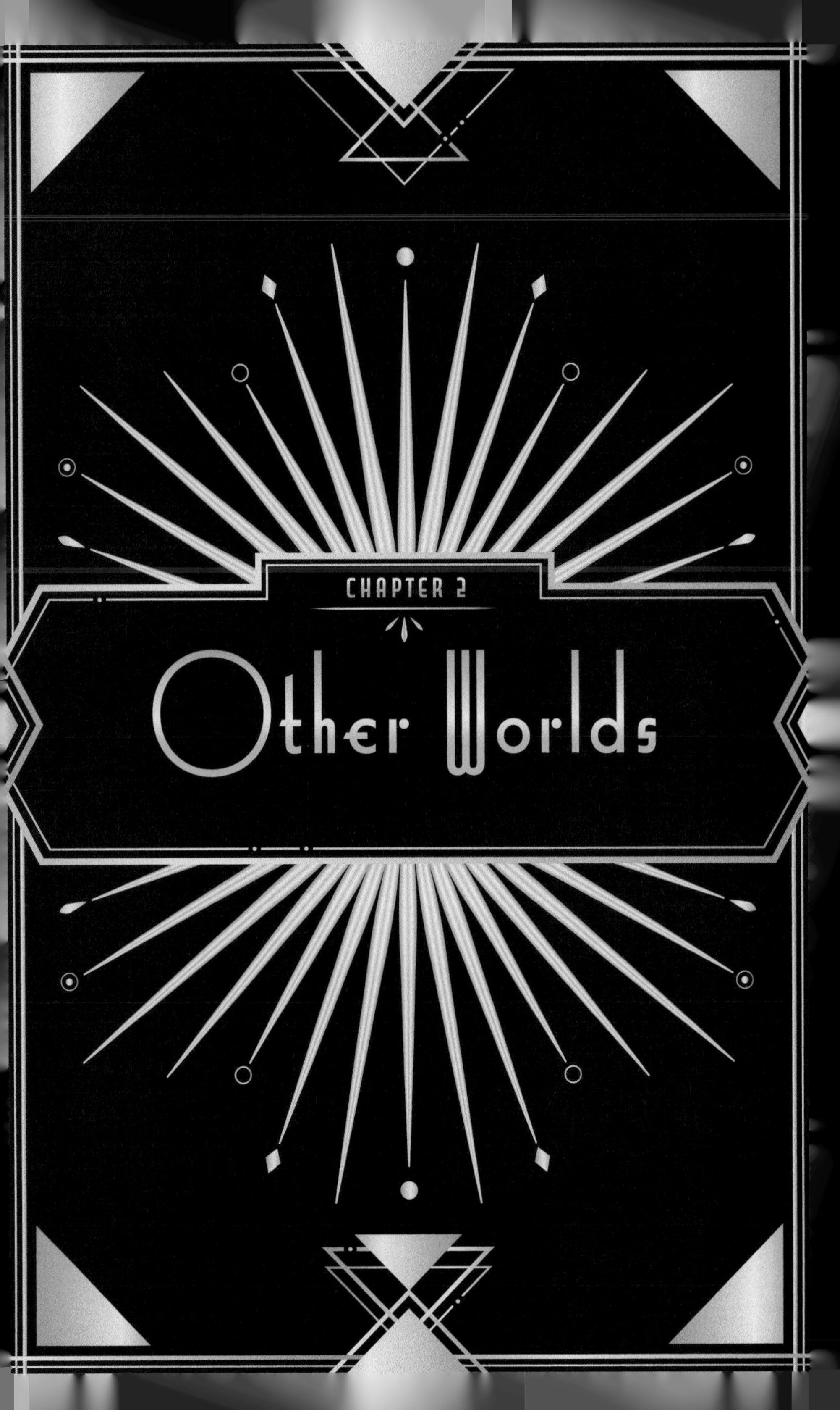

CHAPTER 2

Other Worlds

"Ladies and gentlemen! You came here to be astonished! You came here to be awed!

"And the mighty, the stupendous, the death-defying Flying Graysons delivered!"

Thin crowd again tonight.

It's okay—it's going to be okay. We'll bounce back soon enough.

And Dick—

Good job out there. Way to really hit all your marks.

Oh, yeah. Thanks, Dad.

Are you feeling okay? You seem distracted.

Yep, totally good. Just going to go... hang out.

Well, don't wander ***too*** far.

Things around here are a little... tense.

I promise I won't leave the state.

There was practically ***no one*** in the lion tamer audience tonight.

You see the clown show? Yeah, neither did anyone else.

That carnival—lot of damn nerve putting down their stakes opposite us.

WHEREARE YOUGOING?

AAAH!

Jesus, Willow!

You should ***see*** your face!
But seriously—where are you going?
I'm just going out for a walk.
But ***where?***

Take a guess.
And don't wait up.

"There are other worlds than these..."

Worlds filled with mystery and intrigue. Worlds of unexplainable delights, and unfathomable dangers.
We've seen things you wouldn't ***believe.***
We've seen such beauty as brings men to tears.
We've seen horror that would leave most anyone speechless for all their days.
We've seen the true face of passion and ***love.***
And we're offering it to you, here and now, at...

"The Lost Carnival."
Woooow.

What *is* this place?
A perilous road awaits...
Yes, I can **see** you, young man. And I can see the shape of your most ***fascinating*** future.
Come, let me take a closer look. I can assure you...
My ***cartes du diable*** never lie.
No, ***uh...*** no thank you.
Very well. But just know...
"There is a ***knight*** looming over your days to come."
I'd say all my days have a night, but okay.
There has to be a magic show, or exhibit, or a—
Magic, you say?

Uh... **yeah.** Do you have one here?
Oh yes, you seek Caliban.
Caliban you seek.
But I wouldn't call his performance a **show.**
Oh no, never a show.
Caliban? That sounds... like a **guy.**
A guy, yes.
Most certainly a guy.
Well, do you know where I can find him?
Of course! Caliban only does one performance a night, and it's about to begin.
Follow the crowds...
And follow...
The **glow.**

Ladies and gentlemen, I regret to inform you that due to space constraints, not all of you will be able to attend tonight's performance of Caliban—master illusionist and manipulator of the dark arts.
There will be another performance tomorrow night, so if you are not permitted entry, more opportunities await.
No. Way.
Well—sorry, everybody.
KRRK

And you.
And you.
And finally...

You.

My friends, there was a time before the time we know now. A time of darkness—and light.
It was an era before the crafty ape known as ***man*** surrendered to ***reason*** and banished ***wonder.***
It was a time...
Of ***magic.***
Snap

What in the world...?
Quite stunning, isn't it?
Lodz! I, um...
Didn't expect to see anyone from Haly's? Nor did I. Perhaps it's better neither of us mentions seeing the other?
Uh, sure. The last thing I need is more troub—
Friends, without further ado I welcome you, one and all...
To witness the last magic show on Earth.

LATER.

"And if there's one thing you take away from tonight's performance, let it be this—"

This world is ***not*** the only world there is.

And reality...

This ***can't*** be the end—where ***is*** she?
Is never...

What it seems.
snap

Gasp!
My goodness!

Not to worry, friends. Not to worry.

Those creatures are not of this world—they're merely an illusion. A manipulation of reality.
With a snap of my fingers, they'll vanish as if they were never here.
And so...

Begone, creatures!
Snap
I said begone!
Snap
I said...
I said...
Caliban!
Caliban, are you all right?

It's *her.*

Will you never listen? I've *warned* you about putting on such extravagant performances.
I am too weak. Your magic...*your* magic...
I *can't.* If I use too much it could—*we* could...

You... *must.*
You really don't leave me much of a choice, do you?

Okay, I can do this. Don't push—***control*** it.

Creatures of darkness that are bereft of light—when I snap my fingers...
Disappear into the night.
Snap

As the great scribe once said, a lie well told threatens to outlive us all.
And so, on the path to truth, we sometimes err critically...

And trust in the necessities of falsehoods...
But *always* at our own peril.

What the—?

Excuse me—Caliban! *Um...* Mr. Caliban!

I'm sorry, but Caliban is tired and—wait. You're that guy from the lake.
Yeah, that's me. I mean, I'm him.
I came here from Haly's to see yo—to see the ***show.***
Very nice of you. But like Luciana said...

Luciana.

Right, you need rest. But—those ***creatures*** you made appear.
How did you get one of them to turn into a person?
What?
One of them just...***became*** a person. How does that work?

Do you know what this person looks like?
Um, yeah. Of course.
Then we have to find it...

Before it ***escapes.***

Soooo... that *wasn't* part of the act?
And I'm Dick, by the way. Hi.
That wasn't part of the act. And if I don't catch it before it leaves the carnival grounds... it'll never be returned to where it belongs.
That's bad, right? It sounds— wait.
There—right *there.*
Oh *no.*
It spotted us.
Come on—

We *have* to catch it!
Dick, hurry!
It's almost past the carnival grounds!

I'm *on* it.
Oh no you don't!

Luciana?
Now what do I do?!
Just hold it down! And when I say let it go—
Let it go?!
Trust me. On my word, get off of it...
And get out of the way.

Ready?

Not really!

Well...get ready! And let go...

Now!

ZZZZZNNNGGGHH!

That...
that was *too*
close.

Dick?
Hey—are
you...

Are you all right?
That...that was *intense.* I mean, I've seen magic before. My friend Willow has been sawed in half at least a thousand times. But that...
That was something ***else.***

I know. I mean, nothing around here is exactly... normal. Myself included. Just, please, don't tell anyone about ***any*** of this.
Wait, hold on.

I am ***not*** weirded out. That was ***incredible.***
Really?
I've ***never*** seen ***anything*** like that before.
I've never met anyone like ***you*** before.

I mean, well, *um*—

You're not so bad yourself. The way you helped with those bullies earlier was pretty brave. And...charming.

Charming?

Well, *um*...I should be getting back. People might be looking for me, and—
Getting back? But will I see you again? ***Can*** I see you again?
That's probably not a good idea.
But bad ideas are the most ***fun*** ideas. Maybe...we can have some fun together?
I want to, but it's just that—
Luciana!
I've been looking everywhere for you.
No, just cut right in.
Luciana...
You never answered my question.
Yes I ***did...***

"You just have to find it."
Find it? What does that even *mean?*
Hold on.
No way.

Meet me after
the carnival closes
tomorrow night.
Alone.
YEEESSSSSS!

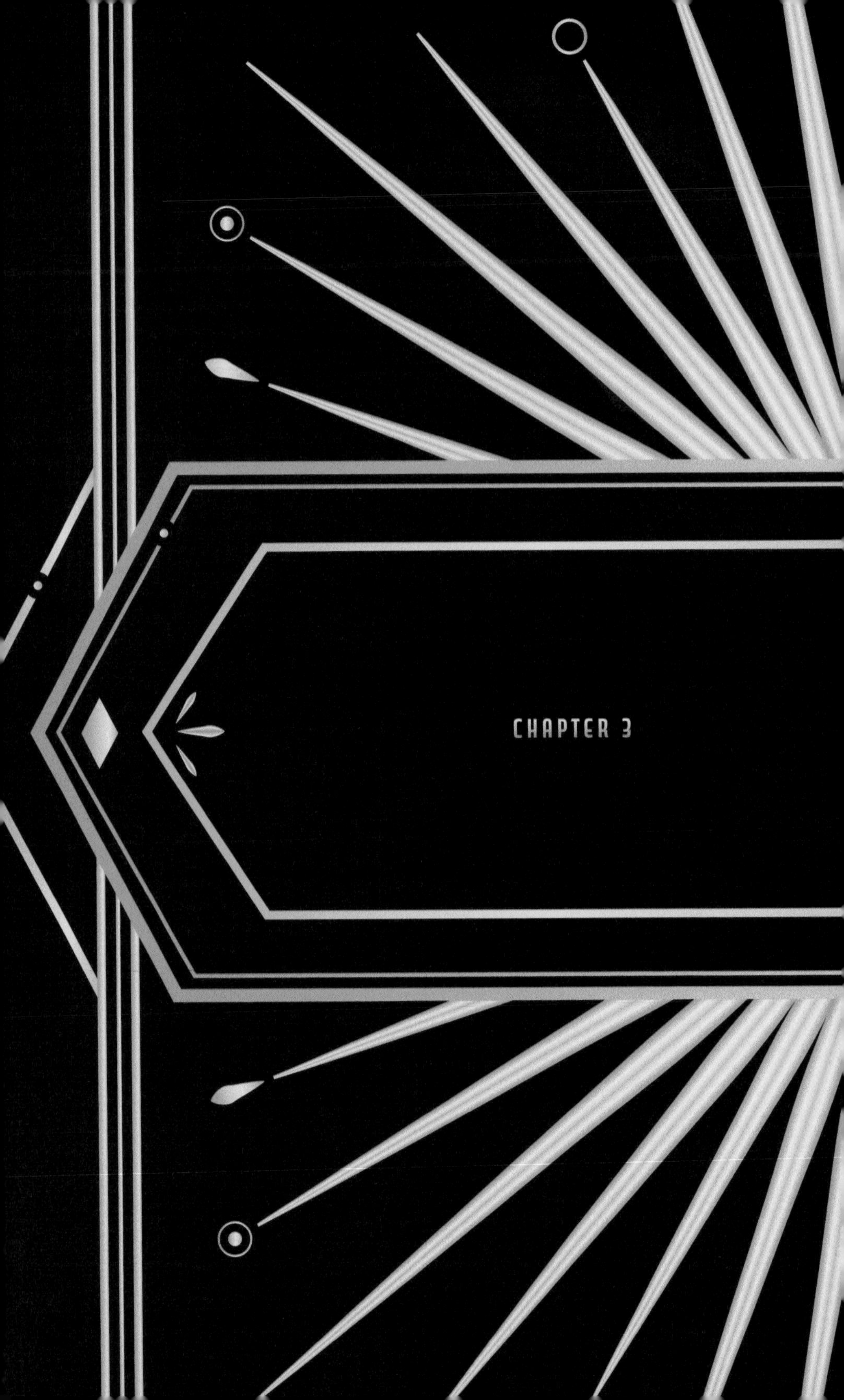

CHAPTER 3

Life is Elsewhere

THE NEXT DAY.

Lodz THE GREAT

Now tell me, young lady, was your card the jack of hearts?

Yeah, but...

Well, that wasn't at all painful to watch.
Lodz'll be fine. He's just taking this whole Lost Carnival thing personally.
But enough about him. As my best friend...
You are obligated to tell me everything.
Um, yeah... okay.
So, I found Luciana, and I ended up helping her with this...thing. She said I was charming, I asked if I could see her again, and—
No—gross. Not your love life, stupid. The magic. Tell me what you learned about her magic.

C'mon, Willow. She's not a...she's not—
A what? A roadside attraction? She is, actually. We all are. Now spill.

Who even said I have anything ***to spill?***
Who do you think? Lodz told me everything about the show, and he also told me he saw you run off with magic girl.
Seriously? He ratted me out?

I'm his protégé and his niece—he tells me these kinds of things. Now are you going to talk, or do I have to stoop to extorting it out of you?

What do you want me to say? Yeah, Luciana does some weird magic—
I'd call it more than ***weird.*** I mean, look at Lodz—he's losing his mind over this.

In case you haven't noticed, I'm not interested in Luciana for her *magic.*
Maybe you *should* be. Because if *I* could do what *she* does, maybe Haly's wouldn't be bleeding customers.
Everything has ups and downs, Willow. Maybe it's a little early to declare bankruptcy?

Do *not* patronize me, Dick Grayson. I know why you're interested in Luciana, but *this* is your home.
This is *not* my home. Home isn't a place that bleeds you dry, then threatens to kick you out the second you step out of line.
Tell me—when was the last time this place cared about what *we* wanted?

You can tell my parents where I'm going. I don't care. But don't try to make me feel like I owe this place a *thing.* I've given Haly more than he deserves...

More than this whole place deserves.

It's okay. You can touch them.

Welllllll...

Maybe I shouldn't?

Don't be timid. *Go ahead*— Amy is absolutely comfortable with it.

Come on, this way—there's *so* much more to see.
Seriously, she's okay, right?
You're sweet—and yes, she's fine.
Dick, this is Claude, our resident escape artist.
Nice to, *um,* meet you. Do you need any help with—
None at all! There's no bind that can hold me down—none but the binds we men place in our minds.
Yeah, totally...
Oh, and over here...
Wild Wilma. The *best* shot west of the Mississippi.
And east, I'd reckon. But that's another story. For now, let me ask...

Enjoy the tour, kid.

This place is ***so*** awesome.

You *really* love this place.
Of course I do. It's my home. Don't you love Haly's?
I don't know. *Maybe?* I've been doing this since I was a kid, and it's been the same since then.
Isn't that how it goes? People go to the same school, live in the same house, see the same people.
Life is repetitious.
Yeah, but change is at least *possible* for normal people. I just don't see a time where I'm doing something *different.*
You know, I haven't even asked—what *do* you do?
Should I?
Wait, you don't *know?*
I mean... yes? But maybe I shouldn't tell you...
Let me *show* you instead.

Take my hand—come on, you can trust me.
Trust you to do what?
Here we go!

There. *That's* what I do.
Throw girls around Ferris wheels?
No, no. I'm an acrobat. My family is the Flying Graysons.
Well, Flying Grayson, you're not too bad.
I sure *hope* not. I was on the trapeze before I could walk.
What you were saying before, about feeling stifled by the circus? I *do* get it. People expect...so much. And before you know it, what they need is more important than what we *want.*
Some days, I just want to walk out of that carnival and keep walking.
Why don't you?
Just know that *you* are not trapped. What you're going through isn't forever. Nothing is.
You just have to hold on to what you have...

Hold on to it for as *long* as you can.

You want to hear something? It's silly, but...

I've never told *anyone* this.

Of course I want to hear it.

When I was really little, my mom took me to a musical. I don't even know what it was, but I remember the lights and the costumes and...the performances. It was *incredible.*

It wasn't a cheap circus act—it was so much *more.* And I've wanted to be part of that ever since. But it'll never happen. It *can't.* It would break my parents' hearts.
But... maybe you're right.

Maybe I'm not as trapped as I think.

So...can I see you again tomorrow?
Um, well—
No—no! You started this!
You started this when you put in your stakes opposite Haly's. There're rules among our kind, and you broke the cardinal one among them.
We're not your kind, and believe me, we have no choice in where we run our operation.
You're taking away our business. Taking food off our tables.
May I suggest, then, that you aim to be more competitive?
Whoa, whoa!

Jonesy, don't!
Dick?!
What're you doing here, kid?
Don't do this. It won't solve *anything.*
No, it won't. But taking these snobs down a peg will sure as hell make us *feel* better.
Look, you might not like it, but these people have every right to be here. Same as we do.
You're kidding me, right?
You're not really siding with *them,* are you?

I don't have to choose. I'm just trying to do what's ***right.***

No, I guess you don't have to choose. It's pretty clear whose side ***you're*** on.
You know what?

My family and I, we're the ones who keep ***your*** stupid circus alive. ***We're*** the stars, which means ***you*** need ***me.*** Not the other way around.

Sounds to me like you've climbed too high on your pedestal, kid—you forget who works on the ground.

Come on, fellas. Let's get out of here.
You all okay? Look, I know Jonesy talks tough, but he's just mad and—
Dick...
You really shouldn't have done that.

Wait, what? I was trying to **help.**
You did, but you also said some pretty mean things to people who clearly care about you.
I didn't want anyone to get hurt. I didn't want ***you,*** get hurt.
You don't even know me. Not really.
But I ***want*** to.
I should get back. And I think you should go home.
Good night.

CHAPTER 4

Fireworks

THREE DAYS LATER.
I once heard a story—many years ago, when I was an apprentice under the Great Mancini.
He told me the legend of a carnival from around these very parts. But there was something strange about this carnival. People said it came from a different time, but it was more than that—
People said it possessed magic. Real magic. Powerful magic!
And this carnival—they say it vanished as quickly as it appeared, leaving no trace in our world.
And you're saying the Lost Carnival is this... out-of-time carnival?
Don't you think it's odd that it appeared from nowhere? Don't you think it's odd what you've seen them do?
ROYAL APPROACH to MAGIC
Darker Magic
THE PRESTIGE

All my life, it's been my greatest pursuit. **Real magic.**
And all my life...

It's remained just beyond my reach.

But even what Luciana can do, it's still an *illusion.* Right?
Are you serious? You think I've been spending all this time honing my craft to do **card tricks?**

No, of course not. But what **exactly** are we talking about?
That, young Grayson...

That is what you ought to investigate.
Find out where this carnival is *from.* Not everything in this world is what it seems.

Is it just me, or is Lodz getting creepier? Your parents are still cool with you spending the summer with him?
He's not creepy, he's just...
Okay, he's creepy. But seriously—
I've been to Caliban's show *twice* now, and there's definitely something to what Lodz says. The magic he does is not *typical.*
So, he's rattled you and Lodz because you can't figure him out?
It bugs me, sure. But that's not what's going on here.
Have you noticed how *strange* that Lost Carnival is? The way they dress, the way they talk. It's just...*off.*
Here we go...
I *knew* this would happen. And that's why I didn't want to come to you and Lodz for help figuring out Luciana.

Excuse me? Look, ***you*** brought this up. Don't get all snippy because you heard something you don't like. I'm just saying they're ***weird.***

And dangerous, according to Lodz. Don't forget "dangerous."

Will you stop being a baby? Lodz is a paranoid shut-in—he thinks hummus is dangerous.

Now, as your ***friend,*** there's something I want to tell you. Can you keep an open mind for two minutes?

Yes, Willow.

I did a little digging at the library in town, trying to fact-check Lodz's story. I ended up coming across something.

Turns out, way back in the 1930s—

BUMP
Whoa, sorry. Didn't see you there, Grayson.

You really did yourself no favors pissing off the crew.

Thank you for pointing that out. I hadn't noticed.

Anyway, back in the '30s, there was this carnival. They did a show around here for the entire summer, every year, for ***years.*** And then, one day...

Poof.
It ***vanished.*** Never heard from again.

It feels like there's something ***more*** to them. Something that maybe we're not seeing.

I know you're trying to help, and I appreciate it. But I can make my own decisions, and right now, my decision is to try to see Luciana again. Somehow.

Then you should probably do that soon. Like, *really* soon.
What? *Why?*
Okay, you did *not* hear this from me but Haly pulled some strings, and he's having the sheriff pay the carnival a visit.
I get the feeling they won't be around much longer.
That slimy piece of—how could he do this?!
Look, if you see my parents, tell them I'm sick or...I don't know. Unavailable.
Grayson, do you even know what day it is?
I have to go, Willow...
I have to *warn* them.

You are not going anywhere.
C'mon, man. I'm here to help.
I think you've helped quite enough already, loverboy.
I get that you're trying to protect your friend, but I'm not—
Not what? Selfish? Reckless? Dangerous?
What? No. I just—I need Luciana.
Not as much as we need her.

But what about what ***Luciana*** needs? Shouldn't she have a say here?

Last chance. If I have to tell you to get lost ***one*** more time, it's going to be with my—

Quinn!

What has gotten into you?
Luciana, I was just—
Speaking on my behalf? Like I don't have a mind of my ***own?***

Fine. But I still think this kid's dangerous, and I'm not going to budge on that. He's nothing but ***trouble.***

I wouldn't say I'm ***all*** trouble. ***Some,*** but Quinn is definitely over—
What are you doing here?

I'm an idiot and shouldn't have talked to the people from Haly's like that. I was frustrated with a lot of things, and it all came out.
Still, I was wrong. And I wanted you to know that how I acted—that's not ***me.***
Well, Dick Grayson...

You may not be trouble—not ***totally***—but you are full of surprises. And that's why I like you.

Oh, and the sheriff! I **really** came to warn you. You guys are in trouble— the sheriff is—
We know. He already came and shut us down— for now.

I swear, if I had known earlier, I would have...I don't know. Done **something.**

I know you would have.

Well, I mean, if that means you have the night **off,** maybe we can...

CRRRKOOOOM
Ooooooh— **that's** what Willow meant.
Meant about what?

It's the Fourth of July. I *totally* forgot.
I don't have a show tonight. And *you* don't have a show tonight.
What do you say we go have some fun?

Well, if nothing else, you've proved me right—
You are most *definitely* full of surprises.

Nah. You travel around enough, and get ***bored*** enough, once in a while you discover cool things.
And you've always done this? Traveled in the circus?
Yep. I was even born in the lion cage.
Really?
No. I mean, I don't ***think*** so.
My parents have been performers their entire lives. My dad was already with Haly's when they met. My mom was part of a local act at one of the circus's summer stops. They fell in love, became a duo, then...eventually became a trio.
That's a nice life story. A little brief, but nice.
I'm lucky— my parents really love each other. And they love what they do. The only problem is...

I don't.
BLOOP
BLOOP BLOOP
How about you?
What's your story?
There's really not much to tell.
Yeah, for sure. Girl with amazing powers from mysterious, fantastical carnival has no interesting backstory whatsoever. That totally makes sense.
Stop. I just—I never think about my past. Everyone at the carnival already knows everything about me.
But I'm not part of your carnival, remember?
Okay.

Well, for starters, I never knew my dad. He died before I was born, and my mom couldn't bring herself to talk about him. It was too painful.

And like your dad, she was always part of the Lost Carnival. It was her life. She and Caliban—he's my uncle, my mom's brother. They used to do a magic act together. But then...

My mom died. She was young and beautiful and then she was gone.
I know she wanted more for me. Better. She wanted me to get away from the carnival, but then things...
Happened. I guess you can say I took her place. And with Caliban, I... I help give the people here what they need.

I'm sorry, Luciana.
No, don't be. I miss my mom— ***a lot.*** But I still have the carnival. I have good people in my life who care about me, and I care about them.
And me.
I hope you know that I care about you, too.
I do.

I had the **same** idea...
But let's just enjoy the fireworks.

You know—you don't have to take anyone's place.
What?
You said you took your mom's place. But you can do what you want. You ***should***—
It's not that easy. Not for me. The carnival, the people ***need*** me.
Yeah, but...

What about what *you* need?
Dick, you have to understand—not everything is what it ***seems.***
Yeah, people keep telling me that.
But why were you at the party? The one where we met.
I...I don't know.
It's a simple question.
I needed to feel like I can exist outside of the carnival, that there's a point where I end and everything else begins.
Exactly. We need to escape, both of us. And I think maybe... maybe we should do it ***together.*** That's what I want.
What do you want, Luciana?

I want... to not think about the past. Or the future. I just want what we have—right **here,** right **now.**

But what if we could have **more?** What if we could be **free?**

Talk? You really expect us to believe you're here to talk?
If that's the case, then why's Annie Oakley packing two rifles? Huh? Explain that.
We came to give you an opportunity to explain why you sabotaged us.
Right—right. And I guess that also explains why your strongman was caught messing with our lion pen.
He's a simple man, and he adores exquisite creatures—which you keep in a foul cage.
And we did indeed come here to talk, though I'm beginning to think you barbarians are incapable of the task.

You want to talk? Let's talk!
OOOF!
POW
CRUNCH
Hey! HEY!

Oh my god.

Guys, stop!
Don't do this!

Kid, I told you before...

Stay *out* of this. Believe it or not, I don't want you to get *hurt.*
Yeah, but I don't want anyone *else* to get hurt.
Dick, for *once,* you just need to listen to what I say and—

OOOF!

KHSSSHH

Dick! Are you okay?
Oh no.
FWOOOSSSHHH

I gotta get some water—find a hose or—
The *fire.* I can't... can't...
Luciana?!
Are you okay? What's wrong?
The flames... they...
Look, I'll take care of it. There's a hose in the animal keep. I'll get that and—
NO!
Don't *leave* me.

That fire will destroy Haly's.
Can you use your magic to put out the fire?
I can't. It's too much.
Luciana, please. There're people here, animals. We have to put this fire out.
I couldn't do it—couldn't save them. Couldn't save...
What? Who?
Everyone.
They're gone, all of them gon—
Luciana!

My sweet girl—it's okay. I'm here. I'll keep you safe.
I didn't do anything, I ***swear.*** She just...what's wrong with her?
Not for you to worry about, young man. Now, if you will stay back...
I'll handle this.

Is she—is she okay? How can I help?
She'll be just fine. But I need to get her back to the carnival. **Immediately.**
Okay, well, I'll follow you and—
Dick! There you are!
I've been looking **everywhere** for you. Come on—you're coming home. **Now.**
No, I **can't.** Luciana, she's—
She's with someone who's going to keep her safe. Just like I need to do with you.
Dick, there is **nothing** more important to me than making sure you're **safe.**
Dad, I know, but...I'm **worried.** I feel like I should be with her.

I get it.
You want to be with Luciana. You want to be doing your own thing. I was your age once too, a thousand years ago. But understand...

What we have here isn't forever. Us being together, traveling and working as a family— this isn't the way it'll always be. I know you don't see it now, but this time is special.
I just want you to know how much your mom and dad love you and—
Johnathan! Dick!

You need to come with me, right away.

Something's wrong with Willow.

CHAPTER 5

I Put a Spell on You

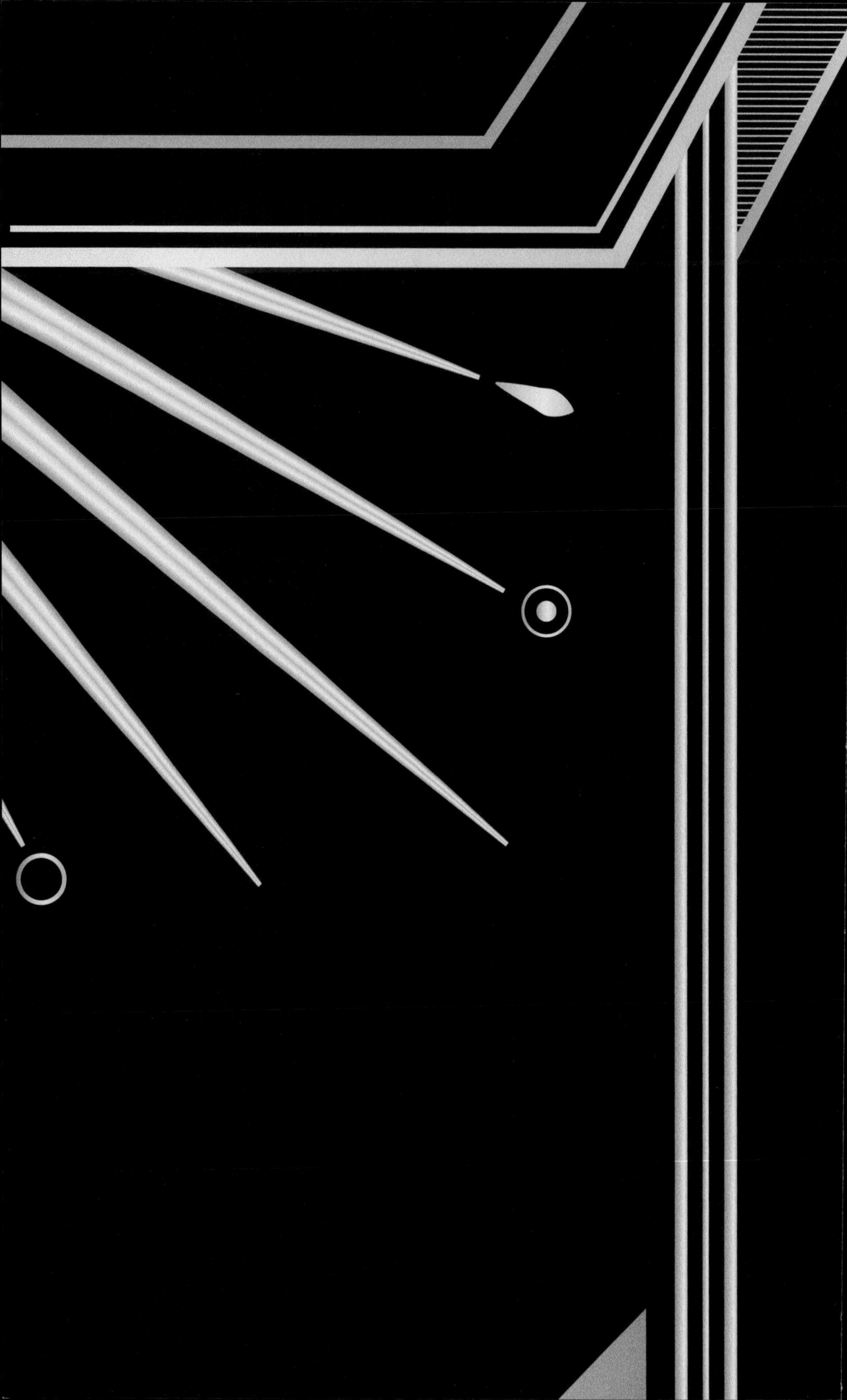

The doc already looked at her, declared her to be in a coma. But I know better—this is no ***coma...***

It's a ***spell.***

A ***what?*** No—no. We have to get her ***real*** help. She needs to go to a ***hospital*** that has doctors who can—

Slow down.

We'll get Willow to the nearest—

No, you can't! I've seen this kind of dark magic before. If you move her, you run the risk of ***killing*** her.

Please—I care for Willow like she was my own daughter. You must ***trust*** me.

And I know of only **one** place such magic could have come from—
The Lost Carnival.
Now wait a second. Before we go throwing around accusations, we should be certain—

Is Willow going to be okay?
Was it really someone from the Lost Carnival that made her sick?

Whoa—hey. Luciana was with me ***all*** evening. And Caliban...he put out the fire. Why would he do that ***and*** hurt Willow? That makes ***no*** sense.

Dick, you and I both know Willow was looking into the Lost Carnival's history. Perhaps she came across something Caliban didn't want found?

I think he **and** his assistant should be made to answer a few questions.
Oh no.
Bring them here—and keep them here until Willow gets better!
Yeah, if they have nothing to hide, they should have nothing to worry about!

No. I will *not* be forced from my home because of some...some... ***accusations.***

Caliban, you don't understand—people are ***angry.*** They think you're responsible for what's happened to Willow.

Can't you just lie low while I clear this up?

Lying low, young man, is the act of cowards and guilty men. I am ***neither.***

Why can't just ***one*** thing be easy?

Listen, if he won't leave, maybe ***you*** still should.

Dick, I can't go. Caliban needs—

With me. Maybe you should leave with ***me.***

I...I...

I *can't.*

The rabble, they...really came.

They ***really*** came.

They *need* me here, and I can't leave.

I can *never* leave.

Willow... I...
LATER.
I don't know what to say. I'm just...

I'm *so* sorry.

This is *my* fault.
If I hadn't gotten mixed up with the Lost Carnival, maybe...I don't know.
Maybe you wouldn't be like *this.*

But I'm not going to let you stay like this— I mean, who am I going to bug if you're not around?

There has to be ***something*** that helps us understand what happened to you.

Some kind of hint or, I don't know, maybe a...

Clue?

Luciana Valde

It can't be.

How *old* is this photo?
Um...what's happening?
Willow?! Anybody?!
I don't like this! I don't—

Oh boy.

Um, excuse me. Can you tell me what—
Aaaaaand I'm a ghost.
Okaaaaaaaaay.
Howard! What can we do?
Grab buckets! Grab water! We have to act before this whole place burns to the ground!
A fire?

Where the hell am I, and how do I make it *stop?*

Go, get the kids out of here! Madame Black's—it's up in flames and the fire's spreading!
But what about you, Dale? This place, it's going to burn.

Can't let this place burn, Lila, it's all we got.
I'll be right behind you.

Now go— get yourself and those kids out of here!
This can't be happening. This can't be *real.*

MADAME BLACK'S
Oh my god.

You guys have to get out of here—*go!* There's no way you can put this out! You're only going to get yourselves hur—

This is all *your fault!*

Hold on—
I'm coming!

Are you *crazy?!* Quinn, do *not* go in there! You'll *die!*

Quinn, you have to *hear* me!

Quinn!

Oh no—no
no no.
QUINN!

Someone—**please!** You have to help him! You have to get him ***out*** of there!

You have to...

Quinn!

Tried to...
tried to...

Quinn, what in the world were you thinking?!

Come on—let's get you out of here.
Couldn't save her...I tried, but...but...
It's okay... it's okay.

Just close your eyes, boy. Everything is going to be okay.
Couldn't save her?
Couldn't save—

Who?
Whoa. Just...
Whoa.
What the ***hell*** is going on?

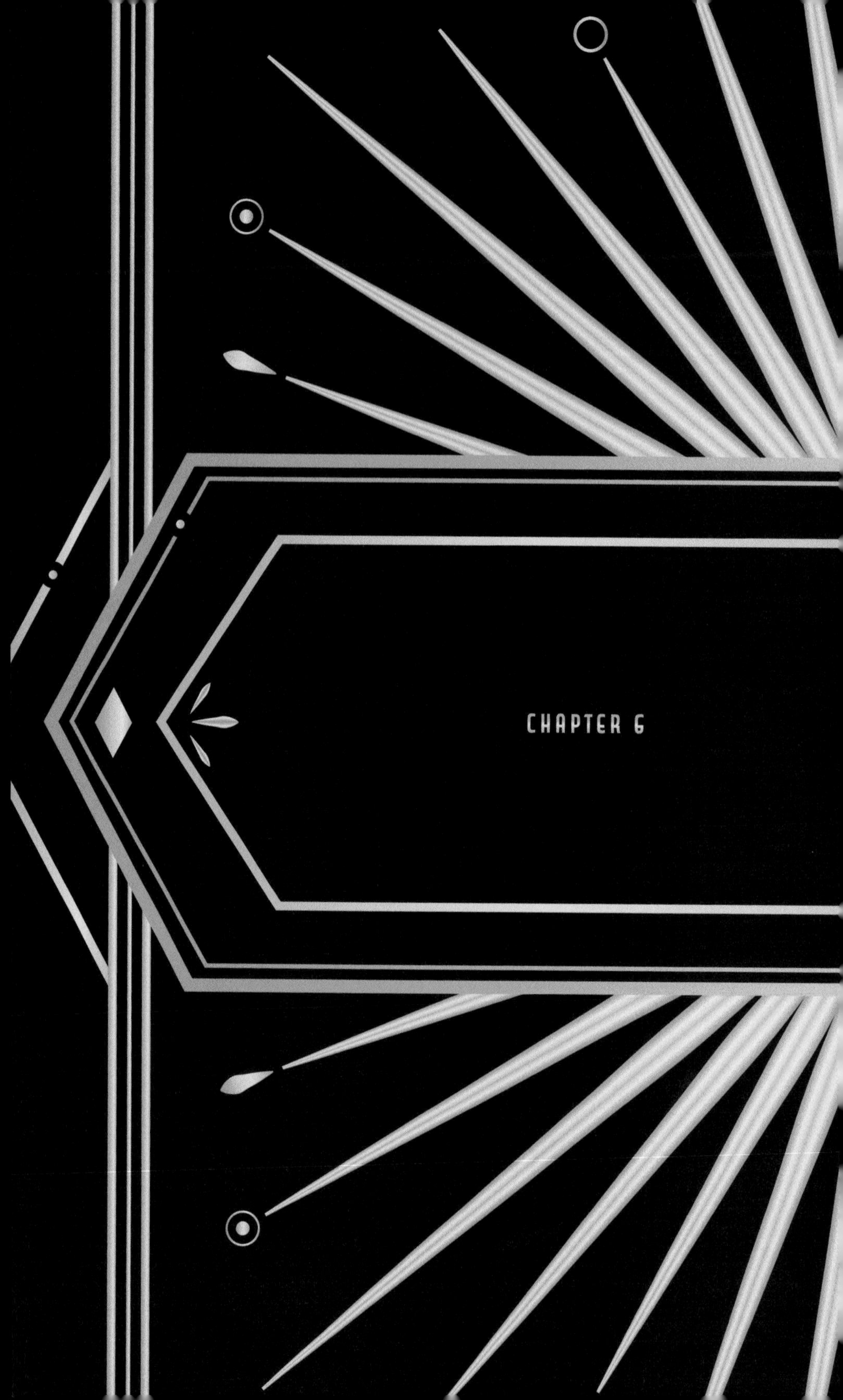

CHAPTER 6

High and Low

THE LOST CARNIVAL.
LATER.

I don't have to tell *you* a damn thing.

You're right. You don't. Because I ***saw*** it. I was there. I mean—I was ***here.*** And...and there was a ***fire.***

Grayson, why don't you go back to the hole you dug up all this dirt from and bury yourself in it?

You don't want to talk about your past—***fine.*** But you will talk about Willow.
Are you joking? I didn't hurt your friend—I didn't hurt ***anyone.***
Really?

Just like you didn't hurt Madame Black?

oOOOF!
Knock it off! Both of you!
What are you *doing* here?

You're *supposed* to be hiding.
And *you* are supposed to be staying out of trouble. And you, Dick Grayson, should be at the circus, helping it recover.
No. I'm not going *anywhere*. Not until I know the truth.
What *is* this place?
I found this book in Willow's tent. And this photo, too. When I touched it, something happened. I was... transported. To here, to *this* carnival.
There was a fire, and Quinn was there, and—
That's enough. I do *not* want to talk about this.

I need to know who Madame Black is. I need to know what Quinn did to her.

Why? What could make knowing that so important to you?
It's important to me because if he ***hurt*** her, maybe he's hurt other people as well.

You think Quinn did something to Willow.

I think there's a lot of mystery surrounding this place. I think I found ***your*** magic book in Willow's room. Since I ***know*** it wasn't ***you*** who put Willow in this coma, it must have been someone ***else.***

I also think you're still not answering my question...

Who's Madame Black?

My mom. Madame Black was my mom. She died in the fire that Quinn started—by *accident.*

Why didn't you tell me this? If you would just explain what all this *is,* I can—
You can what? Change the past? Change my future?

No, but, Luciana, I'm just trying to help my friend.
I know, I know. But this is just...it's too *much.*

It's too *much.*

Care for some company?
Um—yeah... yeah. Sure.

Nice view.
I guess.
You want to talk about it?
I dunno... do you want to listen?

It's not like I've been the best person to you or Dad lately.
You're a teenager—you're ***supposed*** to be a pain in the butt.
Gee, thanks.

Dick, I know your life isn't easy. You're growing up in a circus. Your life is ***nothing*** like those of other kids your age.
Your dad and I knew this would be hard. But we thought that if we loved enough, if we gave enough of ourselves, the things you were missing wouldn't matter.
But...even parents can get it wrong.
Mom, please...

Don't **ever** feel like you've gotten anything wrong.

You okay?
Not really... no.
I'm so scared over what's happening with Willow, and even though I'm sad Luciana doesn't want to see me anymore, I guess I'm **more** sad that I **hurt** her.

Believe it or not, that's a **good** thing.
It means you **care.**

Losing things and having them be lost are very different.
Willow will be okay—I believe that in my heart and soul. And Luciana...

Talk to her. Don't expect anything. Don't want anything. Just tell her what you're feeling, and let her do the same. At the very least...

You can walk away friends.
I still want more. And I can't help but feel she does too. But everything got so...

Complicated.

Believe me, life will do that to you—*relentlessly.* You just have to remember that some things *aren't* complicated, and never will be.
I *love* your dad. That will never change. And if you feel a certain way about this girl, then—
Mary! Dick!
Both of you, please, come quick—it's Willow.
Something's *wrong.*

The magic...it's stronger than I thought. She's fighting it—she's fighting ***hard.***
Nnngggghhh...
But I'm afraid...
Nnngggghhh...
I'm afraid she's ***losing.***
I don't know. This magic is old. It's ***powerful.***
What do we do? Lodz, how do we ***help*** her?!

Then figure it out!

You're the magician—***you're*** the only one who can ***save*** her!

I wish I could—more than anything else, I wish I could.

But I can't.

There's only one person who can help Willow now.

"All right, Grayson. We're here, just like we promised.
Now— what do you *want?*
Good to see you too, Quinn. *Loving* the new attitude.
But I didn't call *you* here—I asked for Luciana.
I need your *help.*

Look—whatever's between us...I'm not here for that. I swear. You can feel whatever you want about me. Hate me if you need to—I probably deserve it. But—
Dick—please stop.
I don't...I could ***never*** hate you. Far from it, and I hope you know that.
No matter what happens.
Luciana, I...there's ***so much,*** but...
I can't. Not right now.
Right now, this is about Willow.

She...
she's ***bad.***
And I
need...well...

I've wanted to help her, Dick. But I was afraid that if we came to your circus— never mind. None of that matters now.
She's here, and I'll do ***whatever*** I can to help her.
Luciana.

I ***will*** help her.

First I need to see ***what*** is happening.

There's definitely a spell over her...it's ***strong,*** and it's... something keeping her...
No.
Oh ***no.***

We have to get her back to the carnival.
We have to get her back there *now.*

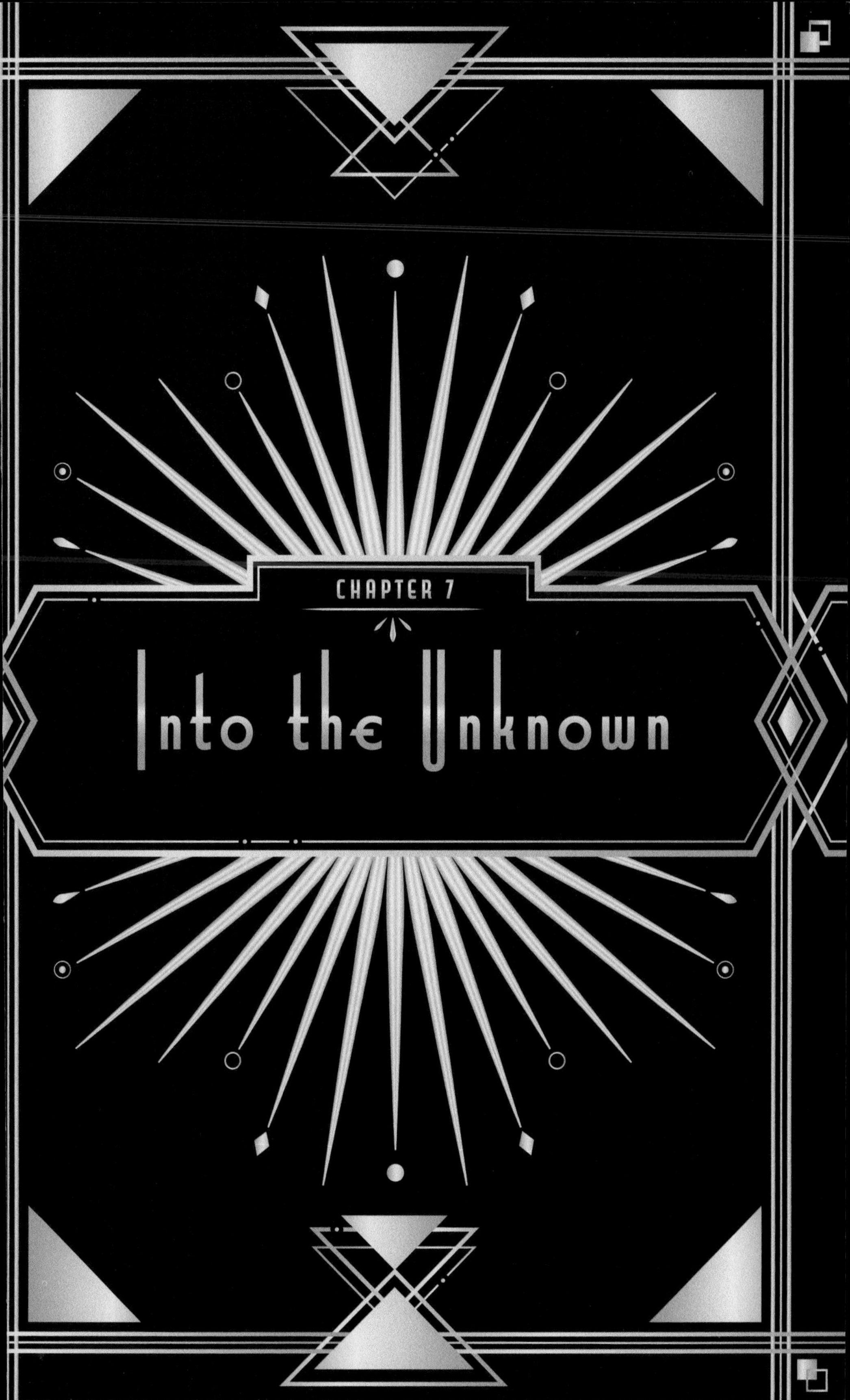

CHAPTER 7

Into the Unknown

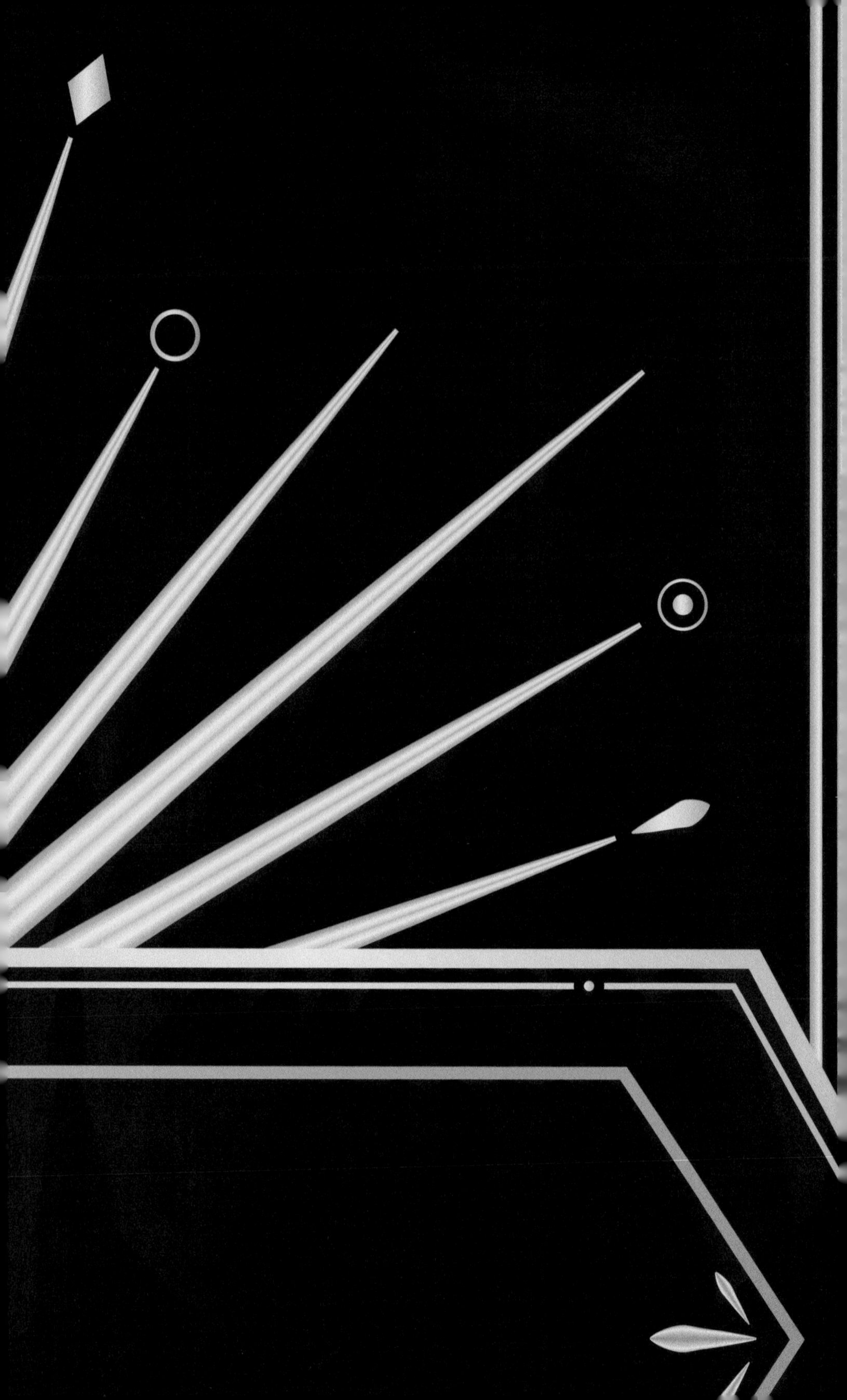

"Okay...okay. Let me get this straight, just one more time.
What you're saying, at least what I *think* you're saying...
Is that Willow is trapped in a...parallel dimension?
I know it's hard to wrap your head around, but there are other worlds than this one. Other worlds where...

Where *other* people live.
The show of mine you came to see. The...creature you helped my niece capture? I summoned him from one such world.
In all likelihood, it is *that* world where your friend has been transported.
Okay— so how do we get her *out?*
I go in and get her.

It's the only way. If I don't go in and pull Willow *out,* she'll never return.

Luciana, you *mustn't!* Think of *our carnival.*

I'm *thinking* of the values you've taught me. Family. Loyalty.

Love.

Always so wise. You make me *proud,* Luciana.

There's no way you're going without me.
And me. I've promised to protect you—even *if* what you're doing is ***insane.***
Thanks, guys.
Very good, but we must hurry. This young lady is fading fast.
Luciana, I'll use my magic to get you in, but it's up to you to get out. And, dear, please—
Be sure to preserve some of your own magic. If you become depleted—
I know, Uncle. It'll be okay.
Go, then. But know that the creatures who inhabit the world you're traveling to, they are hungry for magic...

And *life.*
"And they will ***not*** surrender your friend willingly."

Luciana, are you okay?
I...I'm fine. I just suddenly feel—
Guys, you might want to take a look around...
I don't think Caliban was kidding.
What now?
What now? We kick some ghost ass, get Willow, then we get ***out*** of here.
You really are as dumb as you seem, Grayson. There's no way we take all of them.
No...
We don't ***have*** to.
Quinn— check out your eleven o'clock.

There—that pack of them. None of the others are collected like that. It's almost as if—

They're protecting something.

Or some*one.*

Listen, I'll go around the side and draw a few away. You lead down the middle, with Luciana right behi—

Or we follow Caliban's advice...

And not waste any ***time.***

If we make it back, remind me to knock some sense into you.
Dick! Ahead of you...
When we make it back, you're going to call me your new best frien—
Look!
Oh my god.
WILLOW!
Move... whatever you are!

Willow, come on! Wake up!

Dick—here.
Let me.

Come on, Willow. *Come on.*
Hear my voice. Hear my voice—

And come back.
Come...

Back.
GASP

What is...what is happening? Where am I? I was trapped... like a dream. But then I...couldn't stay awake and—
Dick.

You came for me.
Of course I came for you—you're my best friend.
Now come on. We have to get out of here.

Oh, you're not going ***anywhere.***

None of you are.
What the ***hell?***

For my entire life, I've dreamed of magic like this. I've coveted it, even though I never thought it possible to possess.
But then...
I found you. And you opened the greatest door of my life.
You want my power? Here, let me give it to y—
What is happening? My power, it's...it's...
It's the reason I lured you here.
I put Willow in the coma. I planted the book in her tent. It was I who led you here. And now you're ripe for me to take what's yours and make it mine.
Only one step remains—I must sever you from your magic completely.

Say goodbye, Luciana.
NOOOOO!
NNNGGGGHHH!
Quinn!

Why would you do that?
My...my fault. Y—your mother. It was my...fault.
Maybe now...she'll *forgive* me.
Quinn? Quinn?! No! ***NO!***
Quinn, you can't—

NOOOOO!
Luciana, I know this isn't what you want to hear right now, but we have to do something.
He took everything. My best friend. My magic. All of it—gone.
Not *all* of it.
I'm *coming* for that magic! Let all your friends die for you, I don't care. I *will* have it!
Lodz—I think he has to kill you to get your power. As long as you're alive, you can *stop* him.
I can't dig that deep. If I use all my magic...
I know you're afraid to use your magic, but you *have* to. You're *strong* enough, Luciana.

You might want to take a step back. I've never opened an inter-dimensional portal before...
It might get a little crazy.
Um...

I don't know *what* these things are, but I don't think they're *friendly.*
Uhhh... *no.*

Just fight them off the best you can—we need to give Luciana more *time!*

What the?!

Hello, Willow.
Miss me?
Get off me, you monster!
Luciana! You gotta hurry up!
HELP!
Willow.

Let her go, Lodz!
I'll take her with me, Grayson. I swear I will.
Give. Me. The *magic.*
Got it!
But I can't hold it for much longer...
Take *this* instead!

Willow, go! Get to the portal!
No, it's not ***my*** power you want, fools. It's hers! Get the girl!
I've got ***this.***
OOF!

Always the show-off...
Luciana?
Ready.
Let's go home.

Well, if I've learned one thing...
It's to ***never*** do ***that*** again.
Ooh.
Luciana!

Luciana, my dear—what happened?
I used... too much magic.
I'm losing my hold.
It's okay. Everything's going to be okay.
Come. Let's get you outside, get you some air.
Wait—what's happening? Will she be all right?
You'd better come, too.

What can I do? Should I go get the doctor, or—
I don't think a doctor can fix—
Oh no.
It's all fading away...

How can I...

How can I ***stop*** this?

You ***can't*** stop it.
It's already happening.

No. **No.** There has to be something—***anything***—that will fix this.
We don't belong here. I left this world a long time ago.
But I think you already knew that.

The fire.

All of you...it was the fire.
Caliban saved everyone. Caliban and I, together.
Before the fire could take us, we took ourselves out of ***this*** world. But...

"It takes our magic—
mine, mainly—
to bring us **back.**
"And to keep
us here.

"I can only store
enough magic to
bring some of us
back for a short
time.
"Just so we can
experience life
again, even if just
for a little while.
"Those creatures in the
other world are the few that
I couldn't bring back.

I can't hold
us here forever. I
simply **can't.**
I shouldn't
have gotten close
to you. I'm sorry.
I'm so—

No.
Don't
apologize. Don't
be sorry. I'm not.
Even if I had
known...

I wouldn't have changed ***anything.***
I ***love*** you, Luciana.

Just tell me, when will you be back? When will I see you again?

You won't.
Once my power runs out...it's like I said—nothing is forever.
The best we can do is take things with us and hold on to them...

"Always."

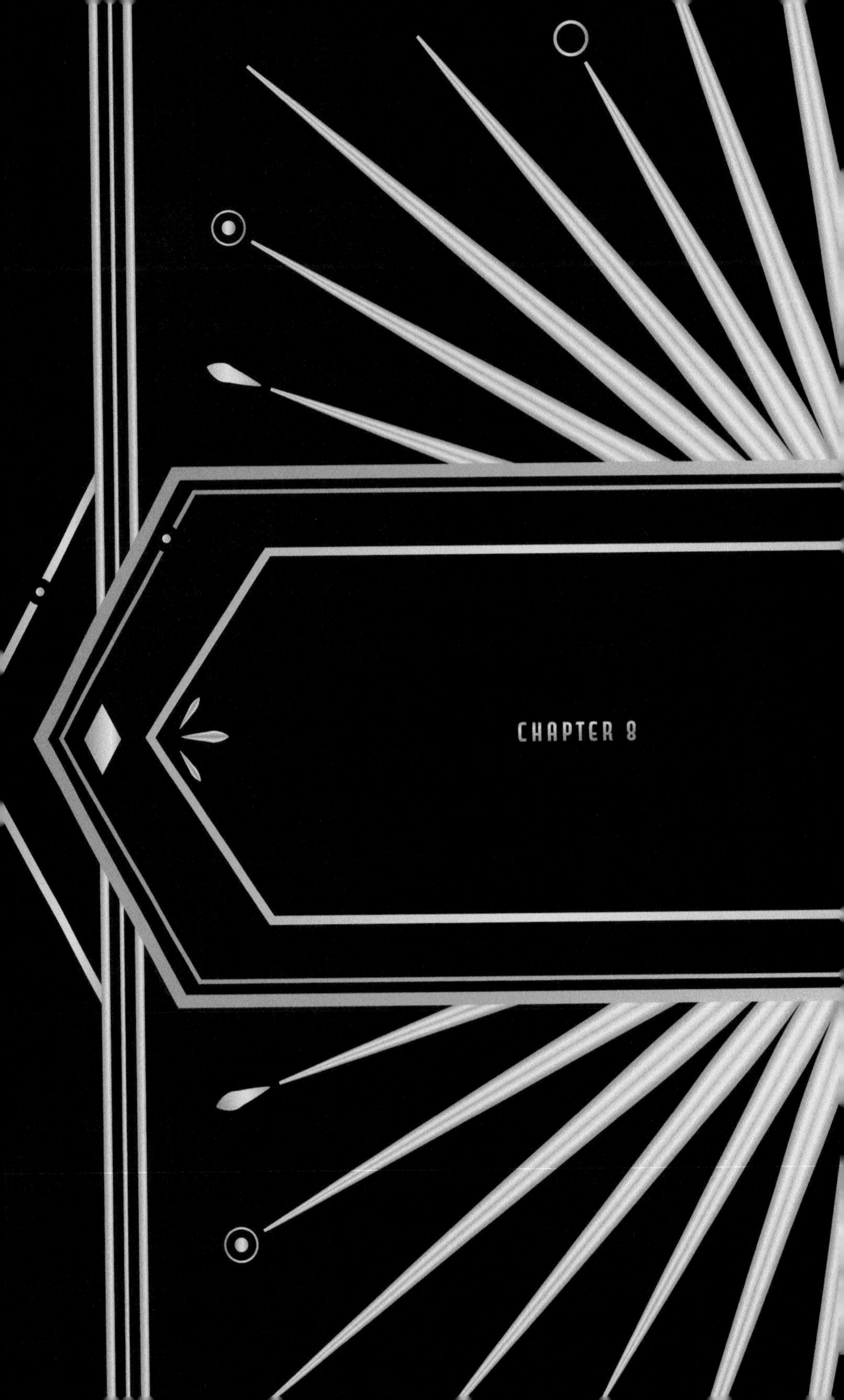

CHAPTER 8

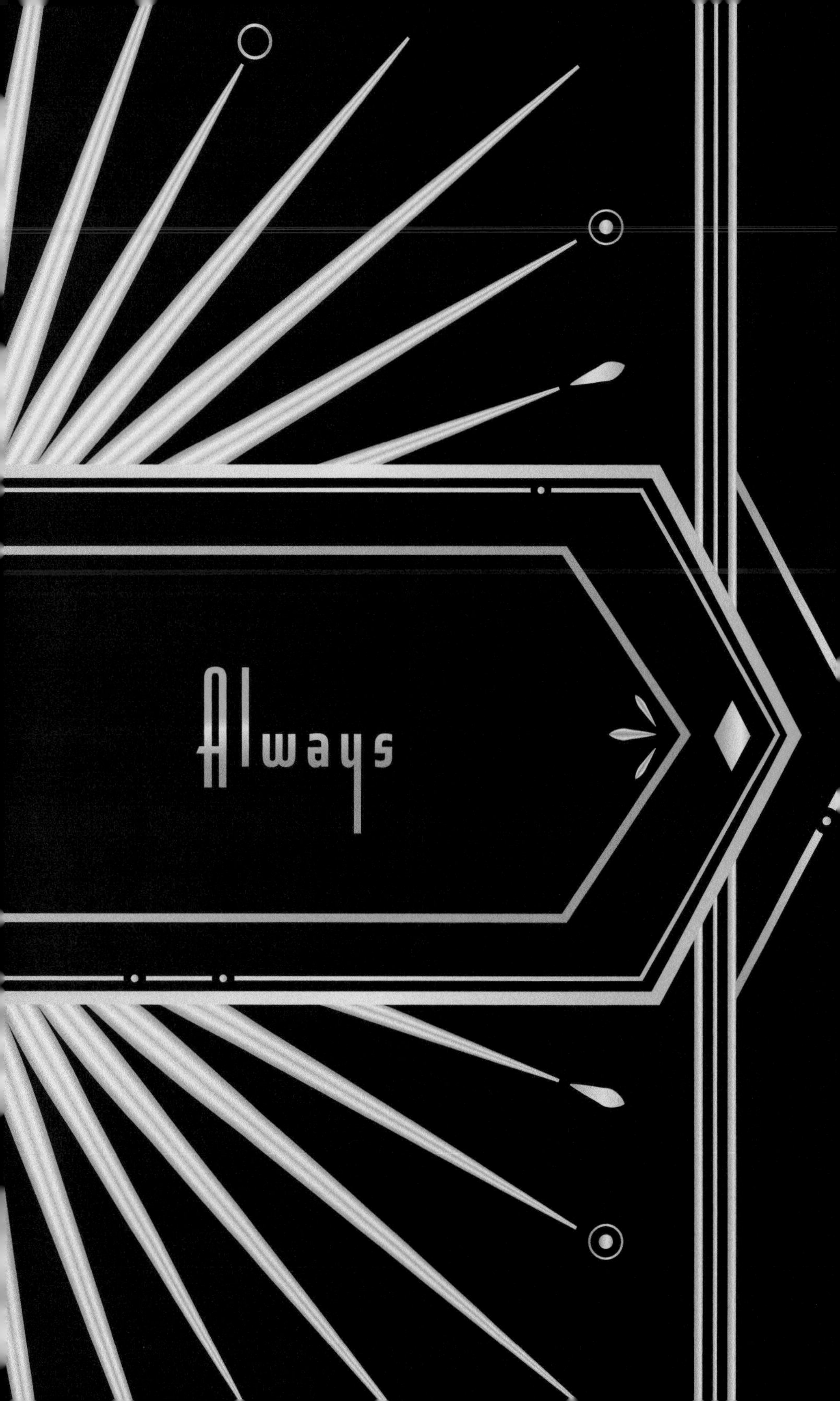
Always

A WEEK LATER.
"Well, life on the road...
HALLY

It sure is *glamorous.*
So...you okay?
I really don't even know. How about you? I mean, you weren't that close to Lodz, but he *was* your uncle...

Yeah, my *creepy* uncle. Who tried to kill me.
So I can't say I'm all that broken up about him being lost in another dimension.
But hey, on the bright side...

Say hello to your new lead magician!

I figured you'd want this.

Well, you ***did*** save me from a parallel dimension, so I ***guess*** we can call it even.
I don't know how I feel about this new, sentimental Dick Grayson.
Oh, don't worry. I'm sure we'll be bickering in no time. But for right now...
I'm just glad you're ***here.***
Yeah, me too.
All right, I'm going to go and finish packing up before we end up writing a poem or something.
And it looks like your ride's here anyway.
14 · H35

We're all packed up, Son. Ready to hit the road?

We...can't imagine how hard this is for you. Any of it.

We can't explain most of this. We probably never will.
But we want you to know that we're here for you.
Always.

I'm sorry.

I haven't been fair to you.
I haven't appreciated our time together as a family.

It won't last forever. It ***can't.***
But I ***want*** to appreciate it. More.

We want that too.
More than ***anything.***

I love you guys. I *never* want to let you go.

Hey, why are we leaving Haly's before everyone else?
Well, we figured we could use some time alone. Just us.
We're taking a vacation. A ***real*** vacation.
We're hitting the road for a week, and maybe we'll stop at a college or two along the way.
We know you don't want this life, Dick. Our life doesn't have to be your life—and that's something we need to learn, too.
"So, what do you say?
"Ready to figure out what Dick Grayson's life will be?"
THE END

Chad Leverenz Photography.

Michael Moreci is a comics author and novelist. His original comics series include *Wasted Space*, *Curse*, *Hoax Hunters*, *The Plot*, and *Roche Limit*, which *Paste* Magazine dubbed one of the 50 best sci-fi comics of all time. Moreci has also written canonical comics for *Star Wars*, *Battlestar Galactica*, *Archie*, and *Planet of the Apes*. His debut novel, *Black Star Renegades*—a space adventure in the spirit of *Star Wars*—was released in 2018 and nominated for an Audie Award; it was followed by a sequel, *We Are Mayhem*.

Sas Milledge is an artist based in Melbourne, Australia. She graduated with a B.Des in animation from RMIT University in 2016 and has since worked in comics, animation design, and illustration both in Australia and abroad. Alongside her own comics and illustration projects, she has completed work for BOOM! Studios, BlinkInk, SparkNotes, 12Field Animation, and the Jim Henson Company.

The Girl Who Refuses to Look Back

OTTO FRIES
What's this? Making your own private Stonehenge?

SKVVNT
Stonehenge is huge.

Really? *Now* you're clamming up?

On se calme, mon pauvre lapin.
That's French for "Calm down, weirdo."

I have a thing for France.
I wish I could go there one day, but...

And I am *so* making sense.
I'm Nora.

And you?

OTTO FRIES
LOVED SON AND BROTHER
TAKEN TOO SOON
1997-2014
Oh, um, my name's Victor.
Enchantée.

Only, I didn't ask what your name was.
I asked who you ***are.***

Well, I'm Nora either way.
C'mon, let's walk!

I told Victor about my mom, how she died when I was ten.
So it's sad being back here, but it's also nice. You know?

Victor's brother is dead, too. He's buried in this same cemetery.
His name was Otto.

As for how Otto died, I have no clue. Victor just gave me the bare bones of the story.
Bones. Ha!

But hey. Respect. A person can be broody or bubbly or whatever...it doesn't matter. Because at the end of the day, aren't we more alike than different?
Everyone has secrets.
To be continued in
Victor & Nora: A Gotham Love Story.
In stores Fall 2020.

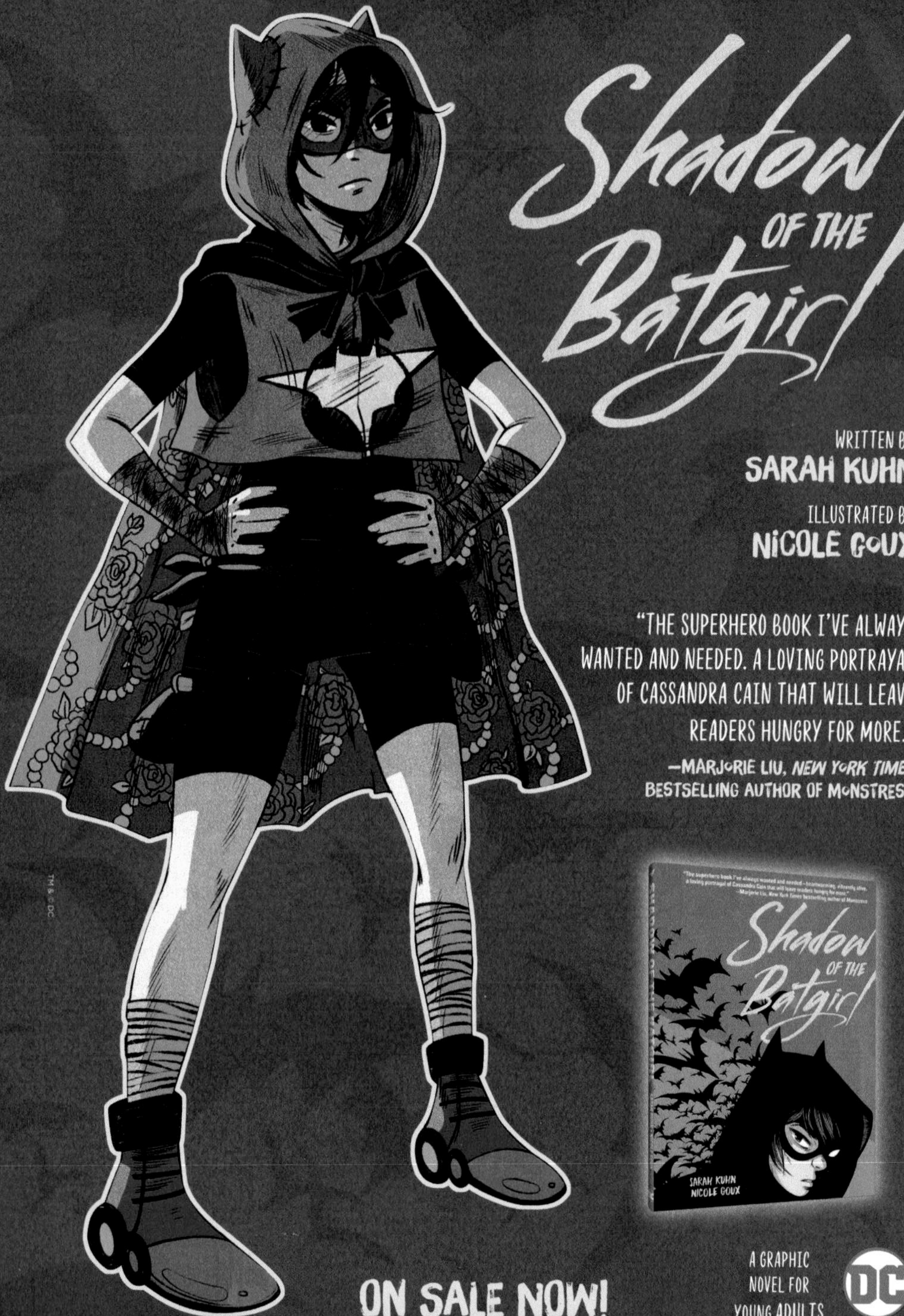

CASSANDRA CAIN—DOING HERO THINGS (OR WHATEVER)
Shadow OF THE Batgirl
WRITTEN BY
SARAH KUHN
ILLUSTRATED BY
NICOLE GOUX
"THE SUPERHERO BOOK I'VE ALWAYS WANTED AND NEEDED. A LOVING PORTRAYAL OF CASSANDRA CAIN THAT WILL LEAVE READERS HUNGRY FOR MORE."
—MARJORIE LIU, NEW YORK TIMES BESTSELLING AUTHOR OF MONSTRESS
Shadow OF THE Batgirl
SARAH KUHN
NICOLE GOUX
ON SALE NOW!
A GRAPHIC NOVEL FOR YOUNG ADULTS
DC
TM & © DC